Anonymous

Three Reports relating to the Hastings Water with an Appendix of Letters

Anatiposi

Anonymous

Three Reports relating to the Hastings Water with an Appendix of Letters

Reprint of the original.

1st Edition 2023 | ISBN: 978-3-38230-386-0

Anatiposi Verlag is an imprint of Outlook Verlagsgesellschaft mbH.

Verlag (Publisher): Outlook Verlag GmbH, Zeilweg 44, 60439 Frankfurt, Deutschland
Vertretungsberechtigt (Authorized to represent): E. Roepke, Zeilweg 44, 60439 Frankfurt, Deutschland
Druck (Print): Books on Demand GmbH, In de Tarpen 42, 22848 Norderstedt, Deutschland

THREE REPORTS

RELATING TO

THE HASTINGS WATER,

WITH AN

APPENDIX OF LETTERS, &c.

ORDERED TO BE PRINTED
BY THE HASTINGS LOCAL BOARD OF HEALTH.

HASTINGS:

GEO. P. BACON, CHRONICLE OFFICE, ROBERTSON STREET.

1859.

CONTENTS.

PAGE

I. Report to the Mayor from the Med.-Chir. Society v

II. Report to the Med.-Chir. Society by the Committee.... vii

III. Report on the Hastings Water by Dr. A. S. Taylor .. xvii

Appendix 1

No. 1. Letter from Mr. Rock to the Town Clerk.......... 1

No. 2. Letter from Dr. Garrett to the Home Secretary 2

No. 3. Letter from the Town Clerk to Dr. Garrett 4

Nos. 4, 5. Letter from the Privy Council Office to the
    Mayor, and Answer thereto 5

Nos. 6, 7. Letter from Dr. Garrett to the Mayor, and Answer
    thereto... 6

Nos. 8, 9. Letter from the Privy Council Office to the Mayor,
    and Answer thereto 10

Nos. 10, 11. Letter from the Town Clerk to the Med.-Chir.
    Society, and Answer thereto 11

Nos. 12, 13. Letter from the Town Clerk to Dr. Garrett, and
    Answer thereto 16

No. 14. Circular issued by the Med.-Chir. Society, and An-
    swers thereto 18

Nos. 15, 16, 17, 18. Letters from the Med.-Chir. Society to
    Dr. Taylor, and Answers thereto 19

No. 19. Letter from the Town Clerk to the Med.-Chir. Society 25

Nos. 20, 21, 22. Letters from the Med.-Chir. Society to Dr.
    Taylor, and Answer thereto........................ 26

No. 23. Letter from the Med.-Chir. Society to the Town
    Clerk 28

Nos. 24, 25. Letter from the Town Clerk to Dr. Garrett, and
    Answer thereto 29

No. 26. Letter from the Med.-Chir. Society to the Town
    Clerk 31

No. 27. Letter from the Town Clerk to Dr. Garrett........ 32

Nos. 28, 29. Letter from the Med.-Chir. Society to Dr. Tay-
    lor, and answer thereto............................ 33

No. 30. Letter from the Town Clerk to the Med.-Chir. Society 34

Nos. 31, 32. Letter from Dr. Garrett to the Mayor, and
    Answer thereto 34

Nos. 33, 34. Letter from the Town Clerk to the Med.-Chir.
    Society, and Answer thereto....................... 36

No. 35 Letter from Dr. Garrett to the Mayor 37

No. 36. Letter from the Med.-Chir. Society to Dr. Taylor .. 38

Nos. 37, 38. Letter from the Town Clerk to the Med.-Chir.
    Society, and Answer thereto....................... 39

I. REPORT

PRESENTED TO THE WORSHIPFUL THE MAYOR
OF HASTINGS FROM THE EAST-SUSSEX
MEDICO-CHIRURGICAL SOCIETY.

Hastings, March 10, 1859,

Sir,

In reference to the Water question. which was referred by the Hastings Local Board of Health to the EAST-SUSSEX MEDICO-CHIRURGICAL Society, we are directed to inform you that the Members have carefully considered all the evidence bearing upon the subject which they have been able to procure, and that they have come to the following conclusions : viz.—

1. That the degree in which the waters supplied by the different Waterworks act upon lead, under the most favourable circumstances, is exceedingly small, being less than that manifested by many soft waters used for the supply of towns.

2. That no authenticated case of contaminated water, fairly drawn from a leaden cistern, has been brought before them ;—that four samples drawn from such cisterns, having been subjected to analysis, were found to contain no trace of lead ;— and that, therefore, in all ordinary cases the water drawn from leaden cisterns in the Borough may be used with safety.

And 3. That no authenticated instances of lead-poisoning from water have been brought before them;—that not one such case has been observed by any of them within the Borough during the past two years;—and that, therefore, any such cases, that may from time to time have occurred, must have been so slight and so rare as to be practically unimportant.

For further details on these points we would refer you to the two accompanying Reports.

We would beg you to bear in mind, that the Members have avoided entering on the abstract question as to the use of leaden pipes and cisterns in general, and have confined themselves strictly to the matter referred to them.

In conclusion, we have only to express to you the gratification felt by the Members at having had it in their power to be of any service to the Local Board of Health, and to assure you of their readiness to give their assistance hereafter, in any matter connected with the sanitary condition of the Borough.

We have the honour to be, Sir,
Your obedient servants,
W. A. GREENHILL,
JOHN PENHALL, } *Secretaries.*

The Worshipful the Mayor of Hastings.

II. REPORT

PRESENTED TO THE MEMBERS OF THE EAST-SUSSEX MEDICO-CHIRURGICAL SOCIETY BY THE COMMITTEE.

In order to assist the Members of the East-Sussex Medico-Chirurgical Society in forming an opinion on the question submitted to them by the Local Board of Health, we have arranged and (with the consent of the Town Clerk,) caused to be printed for private circulation all the letters and other documents relating to the subject. Several of these are totally unworthy of publication, some because they are in themselves quite unimportant, and others because they are in a great measure occupied with subjects entirely unconnected with the matter in hand. Nevertheless it was thought better to print at full length every document at all bearing upon the question, in order to avoid any appearance of concealment by suppressing even those which are in themselves wholly unimportant. Accordingly, we now forward a copy to each Member of the Society for his examination.

At the same time we think it will not be out of place to state at length the course which we have pursued in our enquiry, and the conclusions at which we have arrived; and if the Members of the Society are at first inclined to think that our proceedings have been dilatory (seeing that it is now more than two months since the matter was first brought before us,) we would beg them to look at the dates of the accompanying letters, which will sufficiently show that *we* are not answerable for the delay that has occurred.

But before proceeding further we may perhaps be allowed to remind the Members both of what *has been* brought before us, and also of what has *not* ; for unless this is very distinctly kept in mind, we are likely to be placed in a false position, and to appear to be advocating or defending what we either condemn, or pass over without expressing any opinion on the subject.

In the first place, we were not called upon to consider the purely scientific and abstract question, whether water ever becomes dangerous to health from contamination by lead. On this point there could be no difference of opinion.

Neither, secondly, were we consulted as to whether it would be advisable to discontinue altogether the use of leaden pipes, cisterns, &c., within the Borough. On this point (if we may judge from what has taken place in London and other towns where the question has been discussed by practical and scientific men of great eminence,) it is hardly likely that we should be all agreed ; and even if we were, it would have been impertinent to offer an opinion on a matter about which we were not consulted.

Neither, thirdly, were we called upon to pronounce an opinion on the general quality of the water supplied to the inhabitants and visitors, though this is a most important subject for the consideration of the Local Board of Health, especially when one medical practitioner has been " assailed with the remarks, ' how bad your water is here,' ' the water of Hastings always affects me,' &c., and on inspecting various specimens has found some muddy, some green from filthy tanks, and others positively stinking ;" though he admits that this state of things might " possibly be dependent on the care of the householder."*

But, fourthly, we apprehend that the matter about which we *were* consulted is this, viz. to what amount of danger the inhabitants and visitors of this Borough are at the present time exposed from the use of water passing through leaden pipes and kept in leaden cisterns.

It is to this question that we have strictly confined our attention ; and in order to arrive at a satisfactory conclusion we have endeavoured to conduct our enquiries in an impartial and judicial temper, not wishing to support or controvert any particular " assertion " or " discovery,"

* See Appendix, No. 6. pp. 6, 7

but simply to arrive at the truth, the whole truth, and nothing but the truth, as nearly as the evidence brought before us would permit.

The whole enquiry seemed to resolve itself into the three following questions, which we found to admit of being answered with different degrees of logical and scientific certainty, though for all practical purposes the result is much the same in each: viz.

1. Whether the water supplied to the inhabitants by the different Waterworks * has, in its natural state, such " a peculiar affinity for lead"† as to render it probable that it will become contaminated by passing through leaden pipes or being kept in leaden cisterns ;

2. Whether the water used by the inhabitants of those houses in which there are leaden cisterns, is contaminated with such " a considerable quantity of lead" as to be likely " to produce dangerous disease ;"‡

And 3. Whether, in point of fact, cases of lead-poisoning from water do frequently occur among the inhabitants and visitors of the Borough.

1. With respect to the first point (viz., the quality of the water in its natural state,) one gentleman says § that " it is a notorious fact that the water supplied in these Towns has a peculiar affinity for lead." He also " asserts that the leaden tanks are eaten away rapidly ;" and that "plumbers say that an inch [or *thick*] leaden tank will be eaten in holes in three years," which statement he apparently believes.

In order to ascertain the correctness of these assertions we sent to Dr. Alfred Taylor a sample of water taken

* It would have been manifestly impossible to have extended our enquiries by examining the water of each separate pump or well; and in fact this examination would (as far as our present business is concerned,) have been practically useless, as the water taken from pumps and wells probably never enters leaden pipes or cisterns at all. See Appendix, p. 9. note.

† See Appendix, No. 2. p. 3.
‡ See Appendix, No. 13. p. 17.
§ See Appendix, No. 2. p. 3. and No. 32. p. 35.

Upon the receipt of this Report, so different from what some of us expected, and apparently so contradictory to the results obtained by Dr. R. D. Thomson, we thought it right again to communicate, through the Town Clerk,* with the gentleman in question, in order to give him an opportunity of substantiating his statement, and explaining the discrepancy between the two analyses. As he again declined to avail himself of this opportunity, (although it was proposed that he should take the samples himself in the presence of a competent witness,)† and as we have consequently no accurate information as to how or where his specimens were procured, we shall not attempt to discuss this part of the question any further, but shall simply state that no authenticated case of contaminated water, fairly drawn from a leaden cistern, has been brought before us; and that, until such specimens are produced, we are justified (on Dr. Taylor's authority,) in believing the amount of lead ordinarily present to be " too small to produce dangerous (lead) disease." (p. xix.) ‡

3. The remaining point of enquiry is the most important of all, viz. Whether cases of lead-poisoning from

---

* See Appendix, Nos. 23, 24, 25, 26, 27. p. 28, &c.

† See Appendix, No. 27. p. 32. It appears from this gentleman's last letter to the Mayor (Appendix, No. 35. p. 37.) tha early in December he "sent word to the Water Committee, that, if any one of that body would call upon him, he would shew him the specimens of water he had analyzed, tell him where he had obtained them, and give every information in his power; and that this offer was never accepted." All this, however, took place long before the matter was referred to our Society.

‡ In connection with this part of the subject we ought to mention that it is probable that the number of leaden cisterns within the Borough is much less than was imagined. One gentleman "thinks he is right in saying that forty-nine out of fifty [or 98 per cent.] of the tanks [in dwelling-houses] are leaden." (See Appendix, No. 2. p. 2.) The number of leaden cisterns in St. Clement's parish is 114 out of 166, or only about 69 per cent.: and it is supposed that in the more modern parts of the Borough the proportion is still less.

water are, or are not, of frequent occurrence among the inhabitants and visitors of this place. This is entirely a question of fact, which can be answered only by the aggregate experience of the medical practitioners. One gentleman last autumn "made the discovery that some of his patients were suffering from the poisonous effects of lead ;"* within a short space of time he met with " many cases of colic and other disturbed states of the digestive organs ; he was led to classify such cases, and upon enquiry he found that in all instances where such indisposition occurred leaden tanks were in use ;" he " nearly lost several cases from repeated colic and its consequent innutrition, each one exhibiting manifest symptoms of lead-poisoning; such persons immediately recovered on his desiring them to send for their water from the street pumps, and keeping them on a diet made from that water under their own eyes ;"† he had cases that " were accompanied with tenderness of the abdomen, pain, heat, coldness of the extremities, constipation and fever, which convinced him that a metallic poison was at work."

" On Oct. 4, he was called up at 4 a.m. to visit a gentleman, who had colic in a most violent degree about the navel, and all the symptoms of lead-poisoning," who " had in fact all the symptoms of painter's colic. On the 7th, at 5 a.m., the patient had a second most violent return in an aggravated degree. On the 15th, he was again seized in the same manner with increased ferocity ; again on the 17th, and on the 21st. His health was now fairly broken down, and his medical attendant, as well as his family, began to feel great anxiety, and to despair of his life from extreme exhaustion.... Where to seek for the cause of such renewed attacks the medical attendant knew not, till he tested the water he drank," when " his conviction was sealed in a minute. This was the water he analyzed." The patient " sent for pure water to drink and to have his food cooked in, and had no further attack. He returned

* See Appendix, No. 25, p. 30.
† See Appendix, No. 2. p. 2. and No. 6. p. 7.

to Town, and consulted a physician who has the largest practice amongst the aristocracy of any man in Town, and was met in consultation by another most eminent man. Both expressed their conviction that lead was the cause of the patient's ill health."

The same medical gentleman had " a lady sent by a noble Earl in Sussex to be under his care ; she had similar symptoms, and lost them on having her water from the George-Street pump." He also states that " children have languished in houses where he has found leaden tanks ;" that (about the same time,) " cases were crowding on him....of constipation, and other effects traceable to lead ;"* and that " cases occurred to him here, in which all the symptoms of lead-poisoning became so palpably manifest to him and other physicians elsewhere, that he sought for lead in the water, and he found it."

Though the language of these extracts is somewhat deficient in preciseness, still it is sufficiently alarming, and the general impression meant to be conveyed is abundantly clear, viz. that this gentleman, within a short space of time, met with a considerable number of cases of sickness, occasioned by drinking water kept in leaden cisterns. We wished to learn the exact number of these cases, and if this information had been obtained,† we should have been ready to have received any further particulars respecting them that might have been offered in order to authenticate them. In this instance, however, as in the case of the contaminated water, no information has been given, and therefore the statements must rest entirely on the writer's own responsibility.

In order to discover whether the same symptoms, arising from the same causes, had been observed by the other medical practitioners of the place, we circulated among the Town Members of the Society the following question, viz. " What number of cases of sickness caused by the drinking of water contaminated by lead have you

* See Appendix, No. 6. p. 8.
† See Appendix, Nos. 11, 12, 13; pp. 14, 16, 17.

met with in your own practice during the past two years?"*

Some of us thought it not unlikely that cases of lead-poisoning from water must from time to time have occurred in a place where leaden pipes and cisterns are in use; and if so, it was hardly probable that *all* these cases should have been treated by one and the same practitioner. However, from the answers received it appeared that not one such case had been observed by any other gentleman within the Borough.† We have used the word "*observed*" designedly, because it is important to remember the exact logical value of this testimony; and certainly, if it could be proved that within the last few months there had occurred as many cases of lead-poisoning from water as the gentleman in question believes he has met with, the fact would more than counterbalance any amount of mere negative evidence that could be brought forward. But we would remind the Members of the Society that the existence of these cases has *not* been proved, and that the Informant has declined to produce any evidence of their reality, or to give any information on the subject; and therefore we think, that, until any well-authenticated instances are brought forward, we may safely come to the same conclusion on this point as on the former, viz. that any cases of lead-poisoning from water that may from time to time have occurred within this Borough, must have been so slight and so rare as to be practically unimportant.

We therefore take the liberty of recommending that a short Report be sent in the name of the Society to the Local Board of Health, merely stating the result of our enquiries, without entering into unnecessary arguments or details.

Perhaps we ought to apologize for the length to which these remarks have extended; but they have been written

---

* See Appendix, No. 14, p. 18, and p. 14. notes.

† One Member of our Society had recently met with one case of lead-poisoning by water in a phthisical patient; but this was at Ore, not in Hastings, and the water (which had been noticed by the patient himself,) was rain water kept in a leaden cistern.

with the hope of sparing the Members the necessity of wading through a long, rambling, tedious, and unprofitable correspondence. Our own task has been neither an easy nor an agreeable one ; but, if we have not succeeded in pleasing every body, we have had the consciousness of having endeavoured honestly to do our duty to all the parties concerned in the enquiry.*

(Signed)

> W. A. GREENHILL,
> GEORGE MOORE,
> JOHN PENHALL,
> J. CHARLES SAVERY,
> G. B. TURNER.

Hastings, March 8, 1859.

---

* The following spontaneous expression of opinion on the part of Dr. Taylor makes us hope that we have not altogether failed in this endeavour :—" I have to thank the Secretaries for the very candid and proper manner in which they have placed this matter for investigation before me. It has enabled me with satisfaction to myself to form an unbiassed judgment." (Appendix, No. 29. p. 34.)

III. REPORT

OF EXAMINATION AND ANALYSIS OF CERTAIN SAMPLES OF WATER FROM HASTINGS, BY DR. A. S. TAYLOR.

THE samples of water, well secured and sealed in Winchester Quart bottles, were received at the Chemical Laboratory, Guy's Hospital, on Feby. 1, 1859. The samples were seven in number, arranged in two groups, Nos, 1, 3, 5, and Nos. 2, 4, 6, 7. *Samples.*

They were submitted to a qualitative examination for the detection of the usual constituents of spring and river water. They were colourless, and without smell or taste, —for the most part clear and bright, depositing on standing but a small amount of sediment, chiefly of a silicious or sandy nature. In all the samples, the same mineral constituents were found, namely sulphuric acid and lime, as sulphate of lime,—chlorine, representing common salt or chloride of sodium, carbonic acid and air. *General properties.* *No. 3 deposited the largest quantity.*

FIRST GROUP.

Samples 1, 3, 5.

Of this group, No. 5 was remarkable for its comparative purity or freedom from saline matter. It contained a mere trace of sulphuric acid and lime, as sulphate of lime : the principal mineral ingredient in it, was chloride of sodium, or common salt. No. 1 gave rather stronger indications of the presence of sulphate of lime than No. 5 ; and after 48 hours, there was a visible deposit of the constituents of this substance. The quantity of chlorine or chloride, appeared to be the same as in No. 5. Sample No. 3 contained the largest amount of saline matter of this group. There was a well-marked quantity of sulphate of lime, and a comparatively large proportion of common salt. This water No. 3 also differed from Nos. 1 and 5 in its *Samples 1, 3, 5.* *Saline constituents.*

Saline con-
stituents.
strong alkalinity as a result of the presence of a large proportion of bicarbonate of lime.   No. 5 gave no indications
of the presence of this salt, and No. 1 gave but a faint
trace.   No. 3, however, gave those reactions which generally characterise a water derived from chalk, or a chalky
soil.   Nos. 1 and 5, on the other hand, resembled pure
soft waters derived from beds of sand.

Question
proposed.
     The question proposed for solution respecting these
three waters, which are said to have been taken from
reservoirs, is whether they " HAVE A PECULIAR AFFINITY
FOR LEAD," i. e. any chemical action on that metal by
which effects noxious to health may be produced.

Answer as
to action on
lead.
     The three samples were first tested for lead, in the
state in which they were received.   They contained no
trace of that metal.   Eight ounces of each water were then
exposed in an open jar, in contact with eight square inches
of plumber's lead as it is used for cisterns, the surface of
the metal having been previously cleaned but not polished.
After 48 hours' contact and free exposure to air (circumstances most favourable to the development of any chemical
action of water on lead,) they were examined, with the

Action on
lead.
result that a slight chemical action had been set up in each
case.   This was not rendered visible by any change in the
appearance of the water, although the pieces of lead used
had acquired a whitish incrustation (of hydro-carbonate of
lead,) at the line where the air and water met.   The
waters on being tested for lead, gave the following results.
The maximum effect had been produced in sample No. 5.
The lead here dissolved amounted to about one-fifth of a
grain of the metal in the imperial gallon, or in the proportion of one grain of lead in five gallons of water.   In
Nos. 1 and 3, the action was found to be nearly equal :
it amounted to a proportion of one-eightieth of a grain
of lead in the imperial gallon, or one grain of the metal to
eighty gallons of water.   After the lapse of four days, the
waters, left in contact with lead, were again examined.
There was no perceptible difference in the results.

Conclu-
sion.
     The affinity of these waters for lead, or the degree in
which they act on that metal, under the most favourable

circumstances, is exceedingly small, being less than that manifested by many soft (lake, river, or spring,) waters used for the supply of towns. The chemical action, so far as it went, appeared to have reached its full intensity in 48 hours, and to have then ceased.

SECOND GROUP.

Samples 2, 4, 6, 7.

These waters contained the same mineral constituents Samples as the preceding samples. No. 2 contained a trace of sul- 2, 4, 6, 7. phate of lime, much bicarbonate of lime, and a small quantity of chloride of sodium or common salt. No. 6 contained scarcely any sulphate of lime,—but little lime, and only a small proportion of common salt. No. 7 contained the Mineral in- largest amount of saline ingredients,—the sulphate of lime, gredients. bicarbonate of lime and salt being greater than in any other sample. No 4 came next to No. 7, having more saline matter than Nos. 2 and 6. Hence, of these waters, qualitatively speaking, No. 6 was the purest and No. 7 was the least pure.

The question proposed with respect to this group of Question samples (said to have been taken from leaden cisterns) is proposed. whether they "ARE CONTAMINATED WITH A VERY CONSIDERABLE QUANTITY OF LEAD, SUFFICIENT TO PRODUCE DANGEROUS DISEASE."

Each of the samples was carefully tested at two separate intervals of time for the presence of lead. There was not a trace of that metal in any one sample. A water artificially impregnated with lead in the proportion of one-eightieth of a grain of the metal in a gallon, was tested with them side by side, and the lead in this small proportion was distinctly revealed. Hence it follows that they Conclu- contain no lead, or the quantity present is too small to be sion. appreciated by the most delicate tests, or to produce dangerous (lead) disease.

REMARKS.

When a water in the entire state gives no evidence Remarks. of the presence of lead by a test which will reveal the presence of the one-hundreth part of a grain in a gallon, it may be practically regarded as free from that metal and innoxious. By the concentration of a gallon, it is possible that some traces of lead derived from a leaden pipe or cistern may be found in it ; but in a sanitary point of view, this proceeding is seldom resorted to, aud is not usually considered necessary. The river water of London is occasionally impregnated with traces of lead ; but this is chiefly when it is first used with new leaden pipes or cisterns, or when it contains alkaline nitrates derived from the decomposition of nitrogenous organic matter. It may contain no lead when first drawn from a long used leaden pipe or cistern, but it will act upon and dissolve the metal in small quantity if exposed to a clean surface of lead. I have thus found that the Thames river water supplied to Guy's Hospital, which was entirely free from lead, acquired in less than hour, when exposed to a clean surface of lead, an impregnation of the metal in the proportion of one-eightieth of a grain in the gallon.

Viewing the whole of these samples, the waters from which *à priori* I should apprehend risk of lead-contamination are Nos. 1, 5, 6. A quantitative analysis of these, or of one of these (No. 5) might be desirable ; and if circumstances appeared to justify a still more minute investigation, then I would advise that the samples 1, 3, 5, should be exposed for a longer period of time (a week) in lengths of ordinary leaden pipe as it is used for domestic service. These experiments can be performed if the Local Board of Health desire it. There is enough remaining of each sample for these additional experiments on lead: but should a quantitative analysis of any one sample be required, then it will be necessary that I should receive at least a gallon (two Winchester quarts) of such sample. The proportion of saline matter is obviously so small in the waters designated, that less than one gallon of the water evaporated, would not give satisfactory results.

ALFRED SWAINE TAYLOR, M.D., F.R.S.,
Prof. of Chemistry and Medical Jurisprudence in
Guy's Hospital.
15, St. James's Terrace, Regent's Park,
February 14th, 1859.

APPENDIX.

CORRESPONDENCE, &c.

No. 1.

Letter from Mr. Alderman Rock to the Town Clerk of Hastings.

Hastings, Nov. 20, 1858.

Dear Sir,

Dr. Garrett wishes the Water Committee to see this specimen of water from a lead cistern.* It contains about six grains of carbonate of lead, and is poisonous. He has had some rather bad cases of " lead-poisoning" through water of this kind, and wishes the Committee to encourage, if they cannot compel, the use of slate cisterns.

He was going to send the letter of which I enclose a copy, to the Home Secretary ;† but I told him he had better not send it, except as based on the *general* use of lead cisterns, which are by no means peculiar to Hastings.

Please bring this before the Water Committee to-day, which I am unable to attend.

Yours very truly,

J. ROCK, JUN.

R. Growse, Esq.

* [It is not certainly known how or where this specimen was procured. Mr. Rock states that the quantity of water sent to him was less than a pint ; and that the statement in his letter, as to the quantity of carbonate of lead contained in it, was made upon the authority of Dr. Garrett. The water was afterwards given back to Dr. Garrett, but what became of it eventually is not known.]

† [See No. 2. It would appear from the date of that letter that it had already been sent to the Home Secretary.]

No. 2.

Letter from Dr. Garrett to the Secretary of State for the Home Department. *

(enclosed in the preceding.)

Hastings, Nov. 16, 1858.

Sir,

Permit me to call your attention to the following circumstances, and to solicit your advice on the subject.

The towns of Hastings and St. Leonards are supplied with water by the Corporation†, which is carried in *iron mains*‡ through the streets, but conveyed from them into the dwelling-houses by *leaden pipes*.

From the shortness of the supply the Corporation compelled every house-holder *to provide tanks* for the reception of water for their daily supply. I think I am right in saying that forty-nine out of fifty of these tanks are leaden,§ the slate tanks existing only‖ in private houses.

From the many cases of colic and other disturbed states of the digestive organs I met with, I was led to classify such cases, and upon inquiry I found that in all instances where such indisposition occurred *leaden tanks were in use*.

I have nearly lost several cases from *repeated* colic and its consequent innutrition (in other words, starvation from arrested digestion), each one exhibiting manifest symptoms of LEAD POISONING.

---

* [The copy of this letter which was forwarded by the Writer to Mr. Rock, differs in several passages from the original. We have followed the copy sent from the Privy Council Office, the principal variations being noticed at the foot of the page.]

† [In Mr. Rock's copy the word "chiefly" is added.]

‡ [The *italics*, &c., are used by the *Writer*, not by the *Editors*.]

§ [The exact proportion of leaden cisterns throughout the Borough is not at present known ; but the result of actual enumeration in St. Clement's parish is as follows : viz.—Total number of places supplied with water, 350 ; of which, 114 have leaden cisterns ; 52 have cisterns of wood, brick, or slate ; and 184 have no cisterns.]

‖ [Here the words " (or nearly so)" are added.]

Such persons have immediately recovered on my desiring them to send for their water from the street pumps, and keeping them on a diet made from that water under their own eyes.

I have examined many specimens of water from different lodging-houses, and have found lead in each of them; indeed in one specimen, which I have lodged with the Mayor,* the water looks positively milky from the presence of Carbonate of Lead.† This water is filtered for the use of the house, whereby only the thick portion is removed, the soluble part holding salt of Lead in solution being left for consumption by the inhabitants of the house —visitors as well as the occupiers themselves.

It is a notorious fact that the water supplied in these Towns has a peculiar affinity for lead,‡ which is much increased at this time of year, when a large quantity of vegetable matter in a state of decay impregnates the water derived from the springs, and furnishes in abundance the necessary *Carbon* to unite with the lead in furnishing that deadliest of its salts—*the Carbonate of Lead.*

Plumbers say that an *inch leaden tank*§ will be eaten in holes in three years.‖

As weak persons, (especially those who flock to these towns for health and recovery,) are most amenable to the influences of lead, this is a subject full of *deep importance.*

The Corporation's powers are limited to compelling householders to *provide tanks;* they cannot enforce any particular *kind of tank.* May I ask you, Sir, where powers are to be sought to remedy these evils affecting human life, to which I have humbly called your attention?

* [Mr. Rock, the late Mayor.]
† [Here an "&c" is added.]
‡ [The authority for this statement is not known. The result of Dr. Taylor's analysis is very different: See Report, p. xix.]
§ [Mr. Rock's copy has "a thick leaden tank here."
‖ [We have been informed by plumbers both in London and Hastings that such a thing as "an *inch* leaden tank" is never used in houses; and no instance of even "a *thick* leaden tank" having been "eaten in holes in three years" in this place has been brought before us.]

An early reply will be most thankfully received, as the Water Committee meets on Friday next.*

I am, &c.,

C. B. GARRETT, M.D.

In much haste.

To the Right Hon. the Secretary of State for the Home Department.

No. 3.

Letter from the Town Clerk of Hastings to Dr. Garrett

Hastings Local Board of Health,
Town Clerk's Office, 20th Nov. 1858.

Sir,

At a meeting of the Water Committee held this day, the copy of a letter addressed by you to the Secretary of State on the subject of lead cisterns was read. The Members of the Committee present were of opinion that you could not be aware of the few houses where cisterns are used, certainly not more than half,† within the Local Board District ; and in many instances slate is used instead of lead. Where the latter ones are used, the same are cemented inside, which prevents the chemical action of the water upon the lead.

The Committee attribute the thickness of the water to the boring which is now going on at the Waterworks. Doubtless there are some cases where the cisterns require fresh cementing, which perhaps is the case in some of the houses alluded to in your letter.

I am, your obedient servant,

ROBERT GROWSE, *Town Clerk.*

Dr. Garrett, Wellington Square, Hastings.

* [This last sentence is omitted in Mr. Rock's copy, as is also the postscript.]

† [This statement agrees with the result of the enumeration in St. Clement's parish mentioned above, p. 2. Note §.]

No. 4.

Letter from one of the Clerks in Ordinary of the Privy Council to the Mayor of Hastings.

Privy Council Office, Nov. 26, 1858.

Sir,

I am directed by the Lord President of the Council to transmit to you the enclosed copy of a letter from Dr. Garrett,* and I am to state that his Lordship will be glad to learn from you whether the facts of the case are as alleged; and if so, what course the Corporation propose to adopt for the protection of the health of the inhabitants of the town against the alleged serious danger.

I am, Sir,

Your obedient servant,

WM. L. BATHURST.

The Worshipful the Mayor, Hastings.

No. 5.

Letter from the Mayor of Hastings to one of the Clerks in Ordinary of the Privy Council.

(Answer to the preceding.)

Hastings, Nov. 27, 1858.

Sir,

I beg to acknowledge the receipt of yours this morning, enclosing a copy of a letter written by Dr. Garrett to the Privy Council, and which I shall lay before the Corporation at their meeting next week.

Permit me however to observe that the talented Doctor's views are not by any means in accordance with the official Report of the Registrar-General—the sanitary state

* [viz. the letter marked No. 2.]

of the Borough being, according to the latter authority, in a very satisfactory state, which fact I am fully able to confirm.

I am, Sir, your obedient servant,

W. GINNER, *Mayor*

Hon. W. L. Bathurst, Privy Council Office.

No. 6.

Letter from Dr. Garrett to the Mayor of Hastings.

Hastings, Dec. 7, 1858.

Dear Sir,

I cannot help feeling excessively grieved, and I may say astonished, that an act of mine, which was done with the best and purest intentions, should have been so misinterpreted as to have given rise to the condemnation which I hear has been expressed by members of the Hastings Corporation ; and I must say that I think it is exceedingly indiscreet that any member of that body should be so far forgetful of the interests of the place, as to have made *that* a matter of *public discussion*, which was intended to be strictly private and confidential.

During the enquiry instituted by the Metropolitan Board of Health a few years ago, I collected and communicated to that Board, through Dr. Southwood Smith, a mass of information relating to the action of water on lead, and its pernicious effects on the human system. I saw diseases upon diseases generated by lead—many victims led to a premature grave by its occult, mysterious, and poisoned shafts ; yet the symptoms, causes, and effects had, in many instances, been overlooked, and their identity escaped recognition, and failed to be established.

No sooner did my practice here lead me among a varied class of individuals than I was assailed with the remarks, " how bad your water is here," "the water of Hastings always affects me," &c. ; and on inspecting various specimens I found some muddy, some green from filthy tanks, and others positively stinking. All these facts I passed by, as being of a character [possibly*] dependent on the care of the householder. But I began to find that in cases of irritative indigestion, or weakness of those organs, that symptoms grew up and became manifest, which no previous constitutional condition could account for or explain. Most of them were accompanied with tenderness of the abdomen, pain, heat, coldness of the extremities, constipation and fever, which convinced me that a metallic poison was at work. One specimen of water (corresponding with that I sent to the Water Committee,) I tested, and after evaporating it down, I passed a stream of sulphuretted hydrogen gas through it, and its characteristic dark color was the result—indicating lead.

On the 4th of October I was called up at 4 a.m. to visit a gentleman who had colic in a most violent degree about the navel, and all the symptoms of lead-poisoning. He had been a dyspeptic for years, and was therefore especially obnoxious to the poisonous action of lead. He had in fact all the symptoms of painter's colic. On the 7th, at 5 a.m., he had a second most violent return in an aggravated degree. On the 15th he was again seized in the same manner with increased ferocity ; again on the 17th, and on the 21st. The patient's health was now fairly broken down, and I, as well as his family, began to feel great anxiety, and to despair of his life from extreme exhaustion. Where to seek for the cause of such renewed attacks I knew not, till I tested the water he drank. My conviction was sealed in a minute. This was the water I analyzed. This gentleman sent for pure water to drink and to have his food cooked in, and had no further attack. My patient returned to Town, and consulted a physician who has the largest practice amongst the aristocracy of any man in Town, and was met in consultation by another most eminent man. Both expressed their conviction that lead was the cause of the patient's ill health. A noble

* [This qualifying word was added by the writer while the sheets were passing through the press.]

Earl in Sussex sent a lady to be under my care ; she had similar symptoms, and lost them on having her water from the George-Street pump. Children have languished (one lately from Tunbridge Wells in particular—a medical man came over and fetched the child away,) in houses where I have found leaden tanks.

I much regret that I was led into unintentional error in two or three particulars in my letter to the Secretary of State, but which I corrected *immediately;* and I must say that my informant, from his knowledge of the place, *ought* to have known better.

I mentioned the above circumstances to one of the most talented and esteemed of your Corporation, and asked if the possessors of leaden cisterns could not be *compelled* to change them ? He said, " We can only oblige persons to have tanks, but cannot control the composition of them." Cases were crowding on me (as is usual when autumnal rains wash into the earth the carbon of decomposing vege- table matter, and which readily unites with lead,) of consti- pation,and other effects traceable to lead ; and indeed no varnish can offer protection if the water can reach the lead even through a pin hole. I spoke of these matters to a M.P., (son of one of Her Majesty's Ministers,) and a patient of mine, and he said, "You will be doing the town a great service by writing to the Secretary of State, and ask who has power to alter this state of things. I believe *he* can compel the change of inoffensive tanks for leaden ones." I wrote accordingly, and sent a copy immediately to your late Mayor.

Now I will ask, can the most malevolent and inge- nious mind conceive or invent any intention *I could have had*, or any feelings but those of a philanthrophic and humane character ? Privacy was my object—the pub- licity the subject has obtained, others have to answer for. I being in practice in the place, and being most intimaetly and (for many years) professionally connected with the family of the largest proprietor in these towns, my whole *interest* is to exalt the character of these localities, and to make them as attractive as possible ; and my *duty* is, if there be a black spot, to seize upon it and eradicate it. Let the family of some analytical chemist come down here and suffer from the causes I have alluded to ; he will sound the clarion of alarm, and sweep the very town out. A good and honest citizen will, by forewarning you, forearm you.

Finally, my dear Sir, let me assure you (and I trust this letter may be laid before your municipal brethren,) that, if there is ought to blame in my proceedings, it must be ascribed, as is the truth, to an error of judgment coupled with the best intentions.

A gentleman in the North is about to publish a work on the water supplies of the Towns of England, and their analyses. He applied to me for specimens, and I have forwarded him jars of water from (1) the George-Street pump ; (2) Mr. Rock's factory ; and (3) Spring-Terrace well ; and I believe that these represent the water supplies of Hastings.* I will send the analyses to the Corporation on my receipt of them.

I am, dear Sir, in haste,
Very truly yours,
C. B. GARRETT.

W. Ginner, Esq., Mayor, Hastings.

No. 7.

Letter from the Mayor of Hastings to Dr. Garrett.

(Answer to the preceding.)

Hastings, Dec. 8, 1858.

Dear Sir,

I beg to acknowledge yours of yesterday's date, which I will lay before the Water Committee at their weekly meeting on Friday next.

* [The waters of the George-Street pump and of the Spring-Terrace well probably never enter pipes or cisterns at all, and supply a comparatively small number of families. These three specimens, therefore, can hardly be said to " represent the water supplies of Hastings."]

Your letter to the Privy Council was copied and handed to me by the Lord President's order for the use of the Local Board. I am not aware that it is at all known beyond the parties that it is intended for, or that it has met with any unfair discussion or misrepresentation.

I am, dear Sir,
Your obedient servant,
W. GINNER.

C. B. Garrett, Esq., M.D.

———————

No. 8.

Letter from one of the Clerks in Ordinary of the Privy Council to the Mayor of Hastings.

Privy Council Office, 29th Dec., 1858.

Sir,

I have submitted to the Lord President of the Council your letter of the 27th ult., in which you intimated your intention to lay before the Corporation of Hastings Mr. Bathurst's letter of the 26th ult., and the copy, therein enclosed, of a letter from Dr. Garrett upon the injurious effects of leaden tanks upon the water used in that town and neighbourhood ; and I am to request that you will be so good as to furnish me with the information sought for in the above-mentioned letter from this department, and with such observations upon the subject as the Corporation think proper to offer.

I am, Sir,
Your obedient Servant,
C. GREVILLE.

The Worshipful the Mayor, Hastings.

———————

No. 9.

Letter from the Town Clerk of Hastings to the Lord President of the Privy Council.

(Answer to the preceding.)

Hastings, 18th Feb., 1859.

My Lord,

        I am directed by the Mayor of this Borough to inform you that he has laid before the Hastings Council, acting as the Local Board of Health, the letters dated the 26th of Nov. and the 29th of Dec. last, from the Privy Council Office, on the subject of the injurious effects of leaden tanks upon the water in this town; and the Local Board of Health have caused steps to be taken to have the water analyzed by a competent analyst in London, to whom samples of water have been sent. As soon as the Local Board are informed of the result, they will report thereon to your Lordship; but before doing so, the Local Board wish to be informed whether there is any other communication from Dr. Garrett to your Lordship, the contents of which have not been forwarded to the Board.* At present the Board have only received a copy of one letter dated the 16th of Nov. last.

        I am, your Lordship's obedient servant,

             ROBERT GROWSE, *Town Clerk*

To the Lord President of the Privy Council.

No. 10.

Letter from the Town Clerk of Hastings to one of the Secretaries of the East-Sussex Medico-Chirurgical Society.

Hastings Local Board of Health,

        Town Clerk's Office, 1st Jan., 1859.

Dear Sir,

        I am instructed by the Hastings Local Board of Health to write and ask you to call the attention of the

* [No answer has yet been received to this request, March 2.]

Medical Society in this Borough to a subject which has lately been brought before the Privy Council by a medical gentleman residing in Hastings.

A letter has been written stating that in many houses in Hastings cases of illness have arisen in consequence of the injurious effect produced upon the water by leaden tanks being used.

The President of the Privy Council has written to the Local Board upon the subject, and has requested a report thereon, which the Board intend making ; but before they do so, they would much like to have the subject discussed by those medical gentlemen who belong to the Medical Society, and that they will take such steps as they think necessary to test the water, and ascertain whether or not the leaden tanks produce such an effect upon the water as to be injurious to health.

I shall be happy to furnish you with any further information you may require.

I remain, yours faithfully,
ROBERT GROWSE.

John Penhall, Esq.

No. 11.

Letter from the Secretaries of the East-Sussex Medico-Chirurgical Society to the Mayor of Hastings.

(Answer to the preceding.)

Hastings, Jan. 6, 1859

Sir,

We are instructed by the Committee of the East-Sussex Medico-Chirurgical Society to inform you that the Town Clerk's letter on the subject of the quality of the water supplied to the inhabitants of the Borough, was laid before the Members of the Society at their Annual General Meeting, held on the 4th instant ; and that it shall immediately receive from the Society all the attention which the importance of the subject demands. The matter was discussed at some length last Tuesday ; but, as the Members had not then had any opportunity of fully informing themselves of the facts of the case, a meeting of the Committee was held yesterday for the purpose of considering what steps should be taken.

The Committee are of opinion that further investigation will be necessary before the Society will be able to report on the subject in a manner satisfactory both to themselves and to the Members of the Local Board of Health ; and they require additional information on the four following points before they are prepared to bring the matter again before the Members of the Society for their consideration : viz.

1. The quality of the water supplied to the inhabitants of the Borough generally, both before it enters their houses, and also after it has stood some time in one of the leaden cisterns ;

2. The quality of the water used by the inhabitants of the different houses in which the cases of sickness have occurred, with a distinct specification of each locality ;

3. The experience of each individual Member of the Society as to the amount of sickness caused by lead-poisoning from water during the past two years ; and

4. The number of houses throughout the Borough in which water is kept in leaden cisterns, compared with the total number of houses supplied with water by the different waterworks, with a specification of the localities where most of these houses are situated.

We will take the liberty of saying a few words on each of these points.

1. With respect to the quality of the water used by the inhabitants of the Borough generally, although there may be among the Members of the Society more than one gentleman fully competent to make a chemical analysis (both quantitative and qualitative,) with sufficient accuracy for all ordinary purposes, the Committee are of opinion that on the present occasion it will be advisable (for several reasons which do not require to be specified,) to employ a first-rate analyst entirely unconnected with the place. If this suggestion be adopted, it must be carried out at the

expense of the Local Board of Health, and may be done under their superintendence; if, however, you would prefer that the Medico-Chirurgical Society should undertake the task, the Committee are willing to do so, and to select (subject to your approval,) the chemist to be employed. The Committee will be glad to know your decision on this point as soon as possible, in order that no time may be lost in forwarding specimens of the water for examination.

2. The Committee are of opinion that it will not be sufficient to examine the water supplied to the inhabitants of the Borough generally, without at the same time testing that which is used in each house where any case of lead-poisoning has occurred. It will therefore be necessary for you first to obtain from your Informant a precise specification of each contaminated cistern, and then to procure from each a specimen of the water *in such a state as it is actually used by the owners.* The Committee will also be obliged if you will procure for them the exact number of the individuals seized with symptoms of lead-poisoning during the past two years,* in order that they may be able to compare the experience of your Informant with that of the Members of the Medico-Chirurgical Society.

3. This (viz., the experience of the Members of the Society,)† constitutes the third point of inquiry, and this information the Committee will undertake to procure for themselves. We may be allowed to inform you that the Society comprehends twenty gentlemen practising within

---

* [It was thought that the space of two years was quite long enough for our purpose, as the gentleman who had met with all these cases of lead-poisoning had not been longer resident in Hastings. If, however, we had heard of any cases at all of lead-poisoning from water during that time, we should then have extended our enquiries.]

† [We confined our enquiries to the Members of our Society, because it was manifestly more convenient for us to do so, and the Town Clerk in his letter (No. 10. p. 11.) did not ask us to do more. If, however, (as in the former case,) any of our Members had met with any cases of lead-poisoning from water, we should have consulted the other Medical Practitioners resident in the Borough.]

the Borough ;* and the Committee think that the aggregate experience of all these Members will afford sufficient data for ascertaining the prevalence of any specific disease during the last two years.

4. Lastly, the Committee wish to know what proportion the leaden cisterns throughout the Borough bear to those composed of other materials, in order to enable them to estimate the real amount of danger to the inhabitants from water contaminated by the poison of lead. They also think it will desirable to ascertain the precise parts of the Borough where the leaden cisterns are most in use, in order that they may be able to judge whether all classes of the community are equally exposed to the danger, and have equally suffered from the poisonous effects.† This information the Committee believe that the Local Board of Health will be able to give them, or at any rate to procure for them without much difficulty.‡

We have only in conclusion to apologize for the length of this communication, and to assure you that you shall receive a further report on the subject from the Society as soon as possible.

We have the honour to be, Sir,

Your obedient servants,

W. A. GREENHILL, ⎱ Secretaries.
JOHN PENHALL, ⎰

The Worshipful the Mayor, Hastings.

* [The total number of Medical Practitioners in the Borough is about twenty-seven.]

† [This fourth question was asked by the Committee under the impression that they really would have discovered a certain number of cisterns containing water contaminated by lead. As, however, no such cisterns have hitherto been brought under their notice, the question becomes practically unimportant.]

‡ [This information the Committee has never received, except for the parish of St. Clement.]

No. 12.

Letter from the Town Clerk of Hastings to Dr. Garrett.

Hastings Local Board of Heath,
Town Clerk's Office, 11th Jan., 1859.

Sir,

The President of the Privy Council having requested the Hastings Local Board of Health to make a report upon the effect produced on the Town Water by leaden tanks, I am instructed by the Board to inform you that in order to be able to furnish the Privy Council with such report, the following information is required, which the Board hope you, as the mover in the matter, will not object to give : viz. the precise locality of each house where cases of sickness have arisen with symptoms of lead-poisoning, in order that a precise specification of each contaminated cistern may be obtained, and the Board may procure from each a specimen of the water in such a state as it is actually used by the occupiers of the houses.

The Board wish to be informed of the exact number of the individuals seized with symptoms of lead-poisoning, and attended by Dr. Garrett in Hastings.

I remain, yours faithfully,

ROBT. GROWSE.

P.S. The Local Board hope you will furnish them with the above information at your earliest convenience.

Dr. Garrett.

No. 13.

Letter from Dr. Garrett to the Town Clerk of Hastings.
(Answer to the preceding.)

Hastings, Jan. 13, 1859.

Sir,

I beg to acknowledge receipt of your letter of the 11th inst., in which you request me to furnish the Hastings Board of Health with information relating to the use of leaden tanks at Hastings. Having seen in my professional occupations frequent instances of the injurious and fatal effects of lead-poisoning in years past, my mind has always remained sensibly alive to that insidious enemy.

Cases occurred to me *here*, in which all the symptoms of lead-poisoning became *so palpably* manifest to me and other physicians elsewhere, that I sought for lead in the water, *and I found it !* I therefore became, as you state, "the mover in the matter." To my utter amazement and disappointment I learned that my acts and motives had been violently assailed by some members of the Town Council, and epithets applied to me with a taste I shall not attempt to characterize. In my own defence, I sent two specimens of water taken from leaden cisterns to Dr. R. D. Thomson, of St.Thomas's Hospital, for analysis ; —he "*found them to be contaminated with a very considerable quantity of lead, sufficient to produce dangerous disease, &c.*" *

Take my word for it, that that man is not an honest supporter of the interests of the town who slavers the beauty with flattery and idolatry only, and conceals her imperfections. Let them rather be sought out in a kindly and delicate manner, and be properly remedied. Considering the extremely false and painful position in which I have been placed by some Members of the Municipal body, I beg to decline having my name associated in any manner, for the future, with anything connected with the water supply of Hastings.

I shall, at all times, make it my duty and pleasure to support the best interests of Hastings and St. Leonards, but I shall certainly never again place myself in a similar position to that which I have done in this instance.

I am, Sir, faithfully yours,

C. B. GARRETT.

To the Town Clerk.

* [It is not known how or where these specimens were procured. See below, Nos. 24, 25, 26, 27. p. 29, &c.]

No. 14.

Circular issued by the Committee of the East-Sussex Medico-Chirurgical Society to each Member of the Society practising within the Borough, with the Answers received.

Hastings, Jan. 13, 1859.

Dear Sir,

A question as to the contamination, by lead, of the water supplied to the inhabitants of the Borough having been referred by the Local Board of Health to our Medico-Chirurgical Society, we beg to forward to you (as well as to the other Members,) the subjoined question, and shall be much obliged if you will send an answer at your earliest convenience.

We are, dear Sir, yours faithfully,

W. A. GREENHILL, ⎱
JOHN PENHALL, ⎰ *Secretaries.*

Question.—" What number of cases of sickness caused by the drinking of water contaminated by lead have you met with in your own practice during the past two years ? "*

Answers to the above Question.

None... .. .. .. Charles A. Adey.
Not one. .. .. .. John Wyatt Barnard.
Not one, during eleven Peyton Blakiston,
years I have been in practice   M.D. Cant. ; F.R.S. ;
in the Borough of Hastings.   Fellow of the College
                 of Physicians.
Not any. .. .. .. Roger Duke.
None. I don't think that D. Hoadley Gabb.
this question fully meets the
case.
Certainly not one. .. R. Cooper Gardiner.
None... .. .. .. W. A. Greenhill.

* [Some of the Town Members of the Society have not been resident in the Borough for two years, but they were all resident when the alleged cases of lead-poisoning took place.]

During seven years' prac- A. H. MARKS, M.D., &c.
tice in, and adjoining, this
Borough, amongst the upper
and lower classes, I have met
no case traceable as above—
lead-poisoning only coming
under my notice in those occupied as house or general
painters.

None... .. .. .. GEORGE MOORE.

I have met with no case B. C. PEILE.
of that nature during the
period mentioned.

None... .. .. .. JOHN PENHALL.

I have not met with a FRED. RANGER.
single case.

I have not met with any J. CHARLES SAVERY.
—nor has my Father during
the past thirty years.

Not one. .. .. .. JOS. STEAVENSON, M.R.C.P.

None... .. .. .. FRED. TICEHURST.

Not any. .. .. .. A. TOULMIN.

No case of sickness with G. B. TURNER, M.D.,
symptoms of lead-poisoning   Surgeon.
has come under my notice.

Not any. .. .. .. JOHN UNDERWOOD.

None—but I have only H. LLEWLLYN WILLIAMS,
been in practice in St. Leo-   M.D. Edin.
nards for the past six months.

Not one. .. .. .. ROBT. JAS. WILSON.

No. 15.

*Letter from one of the Secretaries of the East-Sussex
Medico-Chirurgical Society to Dr. A. S. Taylor.*
(Private.)

Hastings, Jan. 13, 1859.

My dear Sir,

The matter of lead-poisoning by water has
been brought before the Hastings Local Board of Health,

who have requested the advice and assistance of our Medico-Chirurgical Society, of which I am one of the Secretaries. We have (among other recommendations,) advised that the water should be examined by some eminent chemist *quite unconnected with the place,* (for, as you may imagine, considerable local feelings and interests are likely to be concerned in the enquiry,) and it is probable that in a few days I may be officially instructed to apply to you for assistance. In the mean time I have engaged to write to you in my private capacity, just to obtain a little preliminary information for the guidance of our Society. Would you therefore be so kind as to tell me,

1. Whether (if the matter should be put into your hands,) you would be able to attend to it at once, as there are several reasons which render it desirable to have the subject examined into as soon as possible :—

2. Whether both a quantitative and a qualitative analysis will be necessary :—

3. What will be the probable cost of making the necessary analysis :—(In connection with this query I ought to say that the Society has proposed to examine not only a certain number of specimens of the water supplied to the inhabitants *generally,* but also the water used in each individual house in which a case of sickness from lead-poisoning is supposed to have occurred.) *

4. How long it will take to examine the waters :—

5. Whether you would prefer coming to Hastings yourself in order to procure the specimens in a fair and satisfactory manner, (which perhaps would in our opinion be the better mode of proceeding,) or whether you would consider this to be beyond your province, and that *your* duty only requires you to examine the water presented to you, no matter how it is procured.—

Will you also add any other hints or information that may be useful to the Committee of our Society at

---

* [The latter part of their intention the Committee have been unable to carry into effect, for reasons to be found below. See Nos. 24, 25, 26, 27. p. 29, &c.]

their next meeting, which is to be held as soon as I receive your answer ?

I need hardly assure you that it is the wish of our Society (and, I quite believe, of the Local Board of Health also,) that the matter should be examined with the greatest candour and impartiality, and I should be sorry if you found a single word in this letter that might lead you to discover my own private opinion on the subject ;—at the same time you will allow me to remind you that the question referred to our Society is not one of mere abstract science, viz., whether the water conveyed through leaden pipes is *ever* injurious to health, (about which there can be no doubt,) but one of practical importance to this Borough, viz. to what amount of danger from this source the inhabitants are at this present time exposed.

Excuse this long letter, and believe me to be,

My dear Sir, yours very truly,

W. A. GREENHILL.

Dr. A. S. Taylor.

No. 16.

Letter from Dr. A. S. Taylor to one of the Secretaries of the East-Sussex Medico-Chirurgical Society.

(Answer to the preceding.)

15, St. James's Terrace, Regent's Park, N.W.,
Jan. 14, 1859.

My dear Sir,

In answer to the inquiries in your letter of the 13th inst., I have to say—

1. That, should the matter be referred to me, I could at once undertake the investigation, and complete it with all reasonable speed.

2. A qualitative analysis would certainly be required ; but the quantitative analysis might be limited to the actual amount of the solid contents in the imperial gallon, and the weight of the *principal constituents* of the water.

3. The customary fee for a quantitative analysis of water is ———; but in this case, the analysis of *each water*, including the search for lead, (the determination of the proportion present, if any,) and the action of the water on lead, would not exceed ———. If more than six waters were examined, the fee for each water above six, would be ———, provided several could be examined at once.

Should, however, the number of waters requiring examination for the Board of Health be so great as to render the expense very heavy, I shall be most happy to reconsider the amount to be charged.

The largest analysis of the kind that I ever had, was in conjunction with my late colleague, Mr. Aikin. We examined for the Corporation of Leicester 42 waters. The customary fees were reduced accordingly.

4. The analysis of one water would occupy two days, as at least half-a-gallon ought to be evaporated : but I can make arrangements by which from four to six waters can be set in operation at once.

5. In cases of great importance to private and public interests, I have generally taken the samples of water myself, or they have been taken in my presence. I have gone as far as Sunderland on a mission of this kind. This, however, is purely a matter for the consideration of those who desire to have the water analyzed. It of course adds to the expense. My customary fee for that is ——— for each day occupied, exclusive of expenses out of pocket.*

In important cases, too, another chemist has been generally associated with me. This is always desirable, where there are funds to meet the additional expense.

In conjunction with my friend Professor Brande I have just completed an analysis of two waters sent to us from Melbourne, in Australia. The enquiry has been a most elaborate one in reference to the action of water on lead. Numerous cases of lead-poisoning have occurred in Mel-

---

* [Upon the whole the Committee thought it unnecessary to incur this additional expense.]

bourne, and are reported to have created great alarm. Our experiments have been carried on from the 8th December, and we have only signed the report to-day, to leave London to-morrow by the mail to Australia. It is a remarkable circumstance to have water sent 10,000 miles for the determination of this question. Our experiments have been on a large scale in leaden pipes—as well as in leaden pipes tinned inside—and in leaden pipes consisting of an alloy of five per cent. of tin and 95 per cent. of lead. We have discovered the cause of the water becoming poisoned. Its composition is almost identical with the Surrey sands water, which led to the poisoning of the Royal Family of France at Claremont.

We have also made the unexpected discovery that lead pipe *tinned inside* is acted upon by the water more powerfully than lead alone. This is owing to the necessary imperfection of the tin lining, and the setting up of a galvanic current by reason of the contact of the water with the two metals. It seems they have been using this imperfect pipe rather extensively.

If the water should be sent to me from Hastings, the bottles should be sealed and labelled by letters or figures. Glass Winchester quarts are the best for this purpose, as we can see the condition of the water. Each Winchester quart holds about from 80 to 90 ounces. The water was thus sent from Australia, and out of twelve bottles only one was broken in transit.

Believe me, my dear Sir, yours very truly,

ALFRED S. TAYLOR

P.S. The question or questions to be answered by the analysis of the water should be clearly stated in writing. The quantity of water of each sample should be at least half-a-gallon, or a *whole gallon* if it could be conveniently sent.

Dr. W. A. Greenhill.

No. 17.

*Letter from the Secretaries of the East-Sussex Medico-
Chirurgical Society to Dr. A. S. Taylor.*

Hastings, Jan. 22, 1859.

Dear Sir,

We beg to inform you that the Hastings Local
Board of Health has referred to the East-Sussex Medico-
Chirurgical Society certain questions relating to the quality
of the water supplied to the inhabitants of the Borough,
especially as to its contamination by lead. The Society
has determined to request you to examine samples of the
water, and therefore we now write to enquire whether it
might not be sufficient to have in the first instance only a
qualitative analysis of all the specimens, and afterwards a
quantitative analysis of those which may seem to require it.
In the case of a qualitative analysis we should be glad to
know what quantity of water will be sufficient for the purpose.

We remain, dear Sir, yours faithfully,

W. A. GREENHILL, ⎱
JOHN PENHALL. ⎰ *Secretaries.*

Dr. A. S. Taylor.

No. 18.

*Letter from Dr. A. S. Taylor to the Secretaries of the
East-Sussex Medico-Chirurgical Society.*

(Answer to the preceding.)

15, St. James's Terrace, Regent's Park,

Jan. 24, 1859.

Gentlemen,

I think that a qualitative analysis of the
samples of water, as suggested in your letter of the 22nd
inst., will be in the first instance sufficient. A selection
for special examination can, if necessary, be subsequently
made.

I do not think that a satisfactory opinion could be given on a smaller quantity than half-a-gallon, *i. e.* a Winchester quart of each sample.

Be so good as to state explicitly in writing, the question or questions to be solved by the investigation. The sample or samples should be addressed to me at the Chemical Laboratory, Guy's Hospital.

I am, Gentlemen, yours faithfully,

ALFRED S. TAYLOR.

Dr. W. A. Greenhill, and J. Penhall, Esq.

No. 19.

Letter from the Town Clerk of Hastings to the Secretaries of the East-Sussex Medico-Chirurgical Society.

(Answer to No. 11.)

Hastings Local Board of Health,
Town Clerk's Office, 24th Jan., 1859.

Gentlemen,

The Local Board of Health have, in accordance with the wish contained in your letter dated the 6th inst., applied to Dr. Garrett (he being the informant,) for a precise specification of each contaminated cistern where cases of sickness have arisen within his knowledge from lead-poisoning, in order that the Local Board might procure from each of such cisterns a specimen of the water in such a state as it is actually used.

The Local Board have received a reply from Dr. Garrett wherein he declines to give the required information,* consequently the Board will be unable to comply with your request on that point; but the Board do not wish the matter to drop, but, on the contrary, to have the water, supplied by the Board, analyzed, as stated in my previous letter to you.† The Manager of the Waterworks

* [viz. the letter, marked No. 13.]
† [viz. the letter, marked No. 10.]

has instructions to procure and furnish you with samples of water both before and after entering a leaden cistern, which he has ready to leave where you may please to direct. He is also going round to the several houses, and ascertaining the number of leaden cisterns in proportion to other tanks, and the several localities thereof. I will hurry him on with this required information.*

I am yours faithfully,

R. GROWSE.

To Dr. Greenhill, and John Penhall, Esq.

No. 20.

Letter from the Secretaries of the East-Sussex Medico-Chirurgical Society to Dr. A. S. Taylor.

Hastings, Jan. 31, 1859.

Dear Sir,

We have to-day sent off to the Chemical La-boratory at Guy's Hospital a case containing seven samples of water,† which we shall be glad if you will submit to a qualitative analysis, at your earliest convenience.

We wish to know (1.) Whether the samples numbered 1, 3, 5, (which are taken from the reservoirs by which the Borough is supplied,) " have a peculiar affinity for lead ?"‡

---

* [This information has never been received. See above p. 2. note §.]

† [The samples were taken by the Manager of the Waterworks, under the superintendence of one of the Members of the Committee. The samples marked Nos. 1, 3, 5 were taken respectively from the Old Town Reservoir, the Well by the Gas-works, and the Eversfield Reservoir ; those marked Nos. 2, 4, 6 were the same waters taken respectively from leaden cisterns at No. 64, High-Street, No. 13, Wellington-Square, and No. 10, Verulam-Place. The sample marked No. 7 was taken from a leaden cistern at No. 31, Wellington-Square, this being the house in which one or more of the cases of sickness occurred, and from which it is supposed (for we have no certain information on the subject,) that one of the specimens was procured that was sent for analysis to Dr. R. D. Thomson.]

‡ [The words used in the letter marked No. 2. p. 3.]

and (2.) whether the samples 2, 4, 6, 7 (which are taken from leaden cisterns,) are " contaminated with a very considerable quantity of lead, sufficient to produce dangerous disease ?"*

We shall be glad to be favoured with any other remarks relating to the samples that may occur to you,— especially whether you would recommend that any of them should be submitted to a quantitative analysis also.

We shall conclude that the samples have reached you safely, unless we hear to the contrary, and remain,

Dear Sir, yours faithfully,

W. A. GREENHILL, } <i>Secretaries.</i>
JOHN PENHALL,</div>

Dr. A. S. Taylor.

No. 21.

Letter from Dr. A. S. Taylor to the Secretaries of the East-Sussex Medico-Chirurgical Society, enclosing his Report on the Hastings Water.

St. James's Terrace, Regent's Park,
Feb. 14, 1859.

Dear Sirs,

I herewith enclose a report of the results of my examination of the waters which you forwarded to Guy's Hospital on the 1st inst.† I shall retain the residues until I hear further from you.

I am, yours faithfully,
ALFRED S. TAYLOR.

Dr. W. A. Greenhill, and John Penhall, Esq.

---

* [The words used in the letter marked No. 13. p. 17.]
† The Report will be found at p. xvii.]

No. 22.

Letter from one of the Secretaries of the East-Sussex Medico-Chirurgical Society to Dr. A. S. Taylor.
(Private.)

Hastings, Feb. 15, 1859.

My dear Sir,

Your Report has safely reached us, and you will no doubt hear from us officially in the course of a few days. In the mean time there is now no impropriety in my saying that the results of your examination of the waters agree with the experience of all the Members of our Society:—indeed the *medical* part of the question seems at present to be so completely set at rest by your analysis and our experience, that I doubt whether it will be considered worth while to carry on the examination of the waters any further.

As the whole of the documents relative to this business are to be printed for local distribution, I should be glad if you would lend me all my letters, (both official and private,) which I will take care to return to you in a few days. I will also let you see a proof sheet of your letters and Report, in case there should be any trifling alteration (whether by addition or omission,) that you may wish to make.

Allow me to congratulate you heartily on the Swiney prize, which could hardly have been more worthily bestowed ; and believe me to be,

My dear Sir, yours very faithfully,

W. A. GREENHILL.

Dr. A. S. Taylor.

No. 23.

Letter from the Secretaries of the East-Sussex Medico-Chirurgical Society to the Town Clerk of Hastings.

Hastings, Feb. 16, 1859.

Dear Sir,

We beg to inform you that we have received

Dr. Taylor's Report on the Hastings Water, and that he has been unable to discover any amount of lead* in the samples submitted to him for examination. Under these circumstances we should be glad to know where your Informant procured the samples of water which he forwarded for analysis to Dr. R. D. Thomson, and which were found to be "contaminated with a very considerable quantity of lead, sufficient to produce dangerous disease ?"

If you can obtain for us this information we will procure samples of water from the same cisterns, and forward them to Dr. Taylor for examination.

We are, dear Sir, your obedient servants,

W. A. GREENHILL, } *Secretaries.*
JOHN PENHALL,

To the Town Clerk, Hastings.

No. 24.

Letter from the Town Clerk of Hastings to Dr. Garrett.

Hastings Local Board of Health,
Town Clerk's Office, 17th Feb., 1859.

Dear Sir,

The Hastings Local Board of Health have taken steps to have the water supplied by the Board analyzed by a competent analyst in London, who has reported that he has been unable to discover any amount of lead in the samples of water sent, which samples were taken from different lead cisterns within the Borough. It is therefore necessary to ascertain where the water was taken from which you state was analyzed by Dr. Thomson, and which was found to be contaminated with lead. I shall

* [As this expression has been misunderstood (see the letters marked Nos. 25, 31. pp. 31, 35.) it may be as well to explain that we referred to Dr. Taylor's words, (p. xix.) " they contain no lead, or the quantity present is too small to be appreciated by the most delicate tests."]

be obliged if you will furnish me with this information in the course of to-morrow morning, in order that no time may be lost in having a final report made to the Privy Council, which report I think it right to inform you will, together with all the correspondence in the matter, be printed, so that in case you wish to see a proof sheet of the printing you can do so on informing me thereof.

Yours faithfully,

ROBERT GROWSE.

To Dr. Garrett, M.D.

No. 25.

Letter from Dr. Garrett to the Town Clerk of Hastings.
(Answer to the preceding.)

Hastings, Feb. 18, 1859.

Dear Sir,

I have to thank you for your note of yesterday's date.

When I first made the discovery that some of my patients were suffering from the poisonous effects of lead, I told a Member of your Corporation the fact ; he informed me that that body had no power to act. As a matter of *pure philanthrophy* I enquired in higher quarters how such an evil could be remedied, and I *privately* acquainted the Corporation with what I had done.

Would any man believe, that, in a place characterized for its piety, I should have been assailed with such ill-feeling as I have met with ? Indeed one Member of the Water Committee, and who adds to his signature " a Member of the Town Council," wrote me such a note as for rudeness, disgusting language, and falsehood, I never recollect to have seen equalled. All balance was then lost. I must either remain the gentleman, and be silent ; or, in order to meet such conduct with proper weapons, become a confirmed blackguard. I much prefer the former position.

You say that " he," the analyst, " has been unable to discover any *amount* of lead."* He therefore clearly discovered *some* lead, and confirms Dr. Thomson's and my own analysis.

I, for one, regardless of the odium which may be showered upon me, will defend the public from lead-poisoning, and fearlessly stand in the foreranks of those who study the public health and the general welfare of our visitors and the inhabitants.

Had the Corporation conferred with me, instead of appealing to the Medical Society for information which *I* alone could give, I would have joined heart and soul in the investigation and eradication of the evil. If the Water Committee is desirous that the invalids who resort to this place *for health*, should drink out of leaden tanks, be it so. I have entirely washed my hands of the whole subject.

As you are going to print my correspondence, I shall be glad to see a proof sheet.

I trust this letter may be added to it.

Yours truly,
C. B. GARRETT.

I must beg of you to excuse my haste in writing this.

Robert Growse, Esq.

No. 26.

Letter from the Secretaries of the East-Sussex Medico-Chirurgical Society to the Town Clerk of Hastings.

Hastings, Feb. 19, 1859.

Dear Sir,

In reference to Dr. Garrett's answer to your letter of 17th inst. communicated to us yesterday, we find no allusion to the principal subject of that letter, viz., the request that he will furnish you with the source from which he obtained the samples of water submitted by him to

* [See note to p. 29.]

Dr. R. D. Thomson. Will you, therefore, again please to direct his attention to this point? and at the same time notify that he is quite at liberty to take the samples himself in the presence of a competent witness appointed by the Local Board of Health.

We are, dear Sir, yours faithfully,

W. A. GREENHILL, }
JOHN PENHALL, } *Secretaries.*

R. Growse, Esq.

No. 27.

Letter from the Town Clerk to Dr. Garrett.

Hastings Local Board of Health,
Town Clerk's Office, 19th, Feb., 1859.

Dear Sir,

I beg to direct your attention to the fact that in your reply to my letter of Feb. 17th, you have overlooked my principal object in writing, which was to obtain from you information as to the sources from which you procured the water submitted by you to Dr. R. D. Thomson.

Should you prefer it, we shall be glad if you will take the samples yourself, in the presence of a competent witness, which shall be forwarded to our analyst for examination.

If in your reply you will name time and place, I will direct our representative to meet you with perfectly new bottles, to be sealed in your presence when filled.*

Yours truly,
ROBERT GROWSE, *Town Clerk.*

Dr. Garrett.

* [No answer was received to this letter.]

No. 28.

Letter from one of the Secretaries of the East-Sussex Medico-Chirurgical Society to Dr. A. S. Taylor.
(Private.)

Hastings, Feb. 19, 1859.

My dear Sir,

I send you a proof sheet of your letters and Report, that you may have an opportunity of making any slight alterations that may occur to you. In the Report the marginal notes will be added hereafter ;—it is for the printer's convenience they are omitted at present. Will you let me have back my letter of Jan. 13, as it is probable that our Committee may wish to print it, in order to show that no private hints were given you as to what was the general feeling here on the subject ?

It is tolerably certain that no further examination of the samples already sent to you will be required ; but it is not yet settled whether any other specimens will be forwarded for analysis.*

I am, my dear Sir, yours very faithfully,

W. A. GREENHILL.

Dr. A. S. Taylor.

No. 29.

Letter from Dr. A. S. Taylor to one of the Secretaries of the East-Sussex Medico-Chirurgical Society.
(Answer to the preceding.)

St. James's Terrace, Regent's Park,

Feb. 20, 1852.

Dear Sir,

I return the proofs corrected. I have put a blank — in reference to the fees: those who wish to know can see the letters.

I return your letters, which please let me have again when the correspondence and Report are published; of which in a printed form I should like to have a copy.

---

* [The latter part of this paragraph was written with the expectation of forwarding samples from the contaminated cisterns.]

I have to thank you and Mr. Penhall for the very candid and proper manner in which you have placed this matter for investigation before me. It has enabled me with satisfaction to myself to form an unbiassed judgment.

Yours faithfully,

ALFRED S. TAYLOR.

Dr. Greenhill.

No. 30.

Letter from the Town Clerk to one of the Secretaries of the East-Sussex Medico-Chirurgical Society.

Hastings Local Board of Health,

Town Clerk's Office, Feb. 26, 1859.

Dear Sir,

       I am directed by a Committee on Waterworks of the Hastings Local Board of Health, held on the 25th instant, to convey to your Society the thanks of that body for the courteous attention your Society has given to the subject of the contamination by lead of the water supplied to the inhabitants of this Borough :—Also to inform you that the Committee have ordered 500 copies of the correspondence entailed by the serious complaints against the purity of such water to be published, together with Dr. Taylor's Report ; and such a number of copies to be presented to the medical gentlemen of the Borough as they may require.

I remain yours faithfully,

ROBERT GROWSE, *Town Clerk,*

(per J. P. S.)

J. T. Penhall. Esq.

No. 31.

Letter from Dr. Garrett to the Mayor of Hastings.

Hastings, Feb. 26, 1859.

Dear Sir,

       A proof has been forwarded to me of 1st, a letter of mine to the Secretary of State ; 2nd, yours to him ; 3rd, of mine to you ; 4th. mine to Mr. Growse.* Now, as this is merely a tithe of the correspondence, may I ask if the whole of my correspondence with the Town Clerk is to be published, or not? 2nd. May I ask you for the Report of your analyst, who found lead, but "not to any amount ?"† (I use Mr. Growse's words.)‡

I shall most certainly follow in the wake of the Water Committee, and, in military language, " take marching step from them." Depend upon it, if necessary, the public shall judge, and, I doubt not, will protect a single philanthropist from the unseemly attack made on him, spurred on by the jealousies and animosity of those who ought to know better.

An answer to these questions and a copy of the analyst's Report will oblige,

Dear Sir, yours truly,

C. B. GARRETT

May I ask you to preserve this note, as I have no time to take a copy ?

W. Ginner, Esq., Mayor.

No. 32.
Letter from the Mayor of Hastings to Dr. Garrett.
(Answer to the preceding.)

Hastings, Feb. 28, 1859.

Dear Sir,

The whole of the correspondence will be published, together with Dr. Taylor's Report. I will take care that you shall have some copies immediately it is out of the printer's hands.

I am, dear Sir, your obedient Servant,

W. GINNER.

C. B. Garrett, Esq., M.D.

* [viz. the letters marked Nos. 2, 5, 6, 13. Proofs of the letters marked Nos. 25, 31, 35, were afterwards forwarded to the writer for correction.]

† [See note to p. 29.]

‡ [Not exactly. See No. 24. p. 29.]

No. 33.

Letter from the Town Clerk to one of the Secretaries of the East-Sussex Medico-Chirurgical Society.

Hastings, Feb. 28, 1859.

My dear Sir,

Can you send me by bearer Dr. Taylor's Report (original,) as I wish to make a fair copy for the Lord President of the Privy Council.

Yours very truly,

JOHN P. SHORTER,

[for the Town Clerk.]

J. T. Penhall, Esq.

No. 34.

Letter from the Secretaries of the East-Sussex Medico-Chirurgical Society to the Town Clerk.

(Answer to the preceding.)

Hastings, Feb. 28, 1859.

Dear Sir,

In answer to your letter of this morning we beg to say that Dr. Taylor's Report is of course the property of the Local Board of Health, and may be used as the Members think fit; but we would take the liberty of suggesting the propriety of not sending it to the Lord President of the Privy Council until you can at the same time forward the *whole* of the documents relating to the Water question, which we hope to be able to let you have in the course of next week.

We are, dear Sir, yours truly,

W. A. GREENHILL, } Secretaries.
JOHN PENHALL, }

John P. Shorter, Esq.

No. 35.

Letter from Dr. Garrett to the Mayor of Hastings.

March 1st, 1859.

Dear Sir,

I wish now to conclude this correspondence, so that you may complete its publication. After writing you my letter of Dec. 7th, 1858, I received a visit from the Turncock,* as the only person the Water Committee could depute to confer with me respecting this most important affair. As the salubrity of particular dwellings was concerned in the subject, I at once declined placing such information in his hands, and in which he concurred; but I sent word by him to the Water Committee, that, if any one of their body would call upon me, I would shew him the specimens of water I had analyzed, tell him where I had obtained them, and give every information in my power. This offer, as you know, was never accepted.† Is it decent or right that in asserting a great principle I should be driven to stigmatize certain houses only? Had my offer been accepted, the truth must have come out. Here was their dodge. I assert that the leaden tanks are eaten away rapidly. Who eats them? The water, clearly. Will any honest man, then, condemn me for *privately* calling the attention of the Water Committee to such a terrible circumstance? Do not all these proceedings bear a construction of an advocacy of leaden tanks and filthy water, as well as of a medical cabal against a successful brother? Mark me, as sure as the God of truth and justice is evidenced in a righteous cause, this cabal will fall back upon those who seek to persecute me. No, Sir; there is too much of the medical influence at work. A surgeon in this town declared that " now we have got our Don of a Doctor, and we will drive him out of Hastings."

---

* [The Manager of the Waterworks,—the same person who was deputed to confer with the Committee of the Medico-Chirurgical Society on the same subject.]

† [It will be observed that this was before the matter was brought before the Society.]

If you of the Water Committee are content to let your visitors drink out of leaden tanks, I say it is the duty of a medical man, who studies the interest of his patients, to stand forward and *protect them*. I say that the keepers of lodging-houses are *great sufferers*. They are *obliged* to give their lodgers the water they receive; and if the Municipal powers do not make an effort to get the leaden tanks removed, then the holders of lodging-houses are *deep sufferers* from causes over which *they have no control*. A more respectable body of inhabitants does not exist than the lodging-house keepers of these towns, kind, honest, cleanly,* and attentive, to a degree that has gained them a wide spread renown; it is a cruelty to them to be made the victims of any such circumstance. This contest, Sir, will much interest the public; for a contest it is, far more than a research after truth.

I am, dear Sir, yours truly,

C. B. GARRETT, M.D.

I beg that this may be sent for publication, and it will be my last communication on the subject.

W. Ginner, Esq., Mayor.

(Immediate.)

No. 36.
Letter from the Secretaries of the East-Sussex Medico-Chirurgical Society to Dr. Taylor.

Hastings, March 7, 1859.

Dear Sir,

We should have written to you sooner but that we have been expecting to have some of the contaminated cisterns pointed out to us, in which case we should have requested you to analyze some additional samples of

---

* [And yet the writer says that " on inspecting various specimens [of water in their houses,] he found some muddy, some green from filthy tanks, and others positively stinking." No. 6. pp. 6, 7.]

water. As, however, we have not been able to obtain this information, we merely write to say that no further examination of the Hastings water will be required at present. We will take care that you shall receive a copy of the Reports, &c., as soon as they are ready for circulation, and remain, dear Sir, yours truly,

W. A. GREENHILL,⎱ Secretaries.
JOHN PENHALL, ⎰

Dr. A. S. Taylor.

No. 37.

Letter from the Town Clerk to the Secretaries of the East-Sussex Medico-Chirurgical Society.

Hastings Local Board of Health,
Town Clerk's Office, March 7, 1859.

Dear Sirs,

I have seen the Mayor this morning upon the Water subject, and he hopes the printer will be able to let you have the Correspondence and Report in print in time to lay before the Board on Friday next. If this is not done, the matter will have to stand over for another month, which, if possible, I should be glad to avoid.

Yours truly,
ROBERT GROWSE.

Dr. Greenhill, and J. Penhall, Esq.

No. 38.

Letter from the Secretaries of the East-Sussex Medico-Chirurgical Society to the Town Clerk.

(Answer to the preceding.)

Hastings, March 8th, 1859.

Dear Sir,

In answer to your letter of yesterday we beg to inform you that there will be no delay on the part of our Society, and that the printer has promised to have the whole of the letters and other documents ready for the Local Board of Health on Friday morning.

We are, dear Sir, yours truly,

W. A. GREENHILL, ⎫
JOHN PENHALL, ⎬ *Secretaries.*

R. Growse, Esq.

GEO. P. BACON, CHRONICLE OFFICE, HASTINGS.